My Little Star

For Steve, with love always ~
J.B.

For Sophie and Grace, with love ~
R.B.

First published in 2007 by Scholastic Children's Books
Euston House, 24 Eversholt Street
London NW1 1DB
a division of Scholastic Ltd
London ~ New York ~ Toronto ~ Sydney ~ Auckland
Mexico City ~ New Delhi ~ Hong Kong

Text copyright © 2007 Janet Bingham
Illustrations copyright © 2007 Rosalind Beardshaw

10-digit ISBN: 1 407 10512 4
13-digit ISBN: 978 1407 10512 3

All rights reserved
Printed in Singapore

1 3 5 7 9 10 8 6 4 2

Papers used by Scholastic Children's Books are made from
wood grown in sustainable forests.

My Little Star

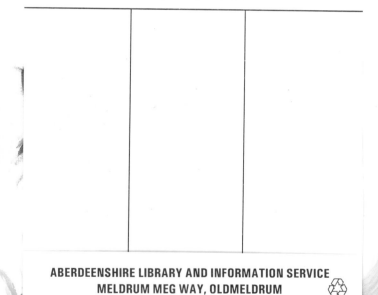

Written by
Janet Bingham

Illustrated by
Rosalind Beardshaw

SCHOLASTIC

Little Fox was chasing falling leaves.
Every time he caught one, another one fell.
"I'm going to catch them all!" he panted.

"It might be hard to catch every one," said Daddy Fox. "There are too many. Look at them all, waiting to fall."

Little Fox stared up at the leafy branches. "Trees full of leaves," he sang, "right up high to the top of the sky!"

"Not quite to the top," said Daddy Fox, tickling Little Fox's nose. "The sky doesn't stop there. Something goes even higher than the trees."

"What goes higher?" asked Little Fox.

"Bees!" said Daddy Fox.
"Watch them!"
A family of bees
bumbled away, over
the top of the trees.

"Bzzzz," said Little Fox.
"I'm a bee, buzz, buzz,
buzzing at the top of
the sky!"

"So does the sky stop there?" Little Fox asked.
Daddy Fox whisked away a nosy bumblebee.
"No, not there," he said. "What flies higher
than the bees? Do you know?"

"Birds go higher!" shouted Little Fox.
"And I'm a bird, flying high to
the top of the sky!"

Little Fox landed with a bump.
  "Is that the top?" he asked.
"Does the sky
stop there?"

Daddy Fox kissed him better.
  "No, not there," he said. "What
      goes higher than the birds,
        but only after rain?"

"The rainbow!" laughed Little Fox. "Look at me now! I'm dancing on the rainbow, up above all the birds and the bees and the trees.

"Is that the top?" he asked. "Does the sky stop there?"

Daddy Fox shook his head. "Something goes higher then the rainbow," he said.

"What does?" asked Little Fox. "Tell me, Daddy!"

"Clouds!" said Daddy Fox.
"The clouds float high and far.
And look, they are showing us
the way home."

Little Fox watched the clouds drifting by.
 "Let's follow them!" he cried and he set off
running and tumbling towards the den.

The sun was setting by the time they reached home.

"Goodnight, Sun!" said Little Fox. "I know you go higher than the clouds, but you're not high now."

"That's true," said Daddy Fox. "The sun is going to bed, just like you. It will climb high in the sky again tomorrow.
But look . . .

"Here comes the moon
to shine in its place." Little Fox
watched the moon brighten overhead.
"I can almost touch it," he said,
"even though it's so high.

"That must be the top," Little Fox said. "Does the sky stop there?"

"No, not there," said Daddy Fox. "What do you think shines even higher than the moon?"

Little Fox looked around the darkening sky.
"Stars!" he laughed. "The stars shine higher."
He started to count them as they turned on their
lights. "So many stars!" he sighed.

"So many beautiful stars," agreed Daddy Fox.

Little Fox yawned. "So that's the top," he said. "The sky stops there."

"Not even there," said Daddy Fox. "You see, there is no top . . .

"The stars shine down from the deep,
dark, quiet space that goes on and on forever."
Little Fox gazed up into the velvet darkness.
He felt warm and safe with Daddy Fox beside him.
"So the sky goes on and on forever,"
he whispered sleepily. "But where does it start?"

Daddy Fox hugged him closer.
"The sky is just like love," he said.
"It goes on and on forever . . .

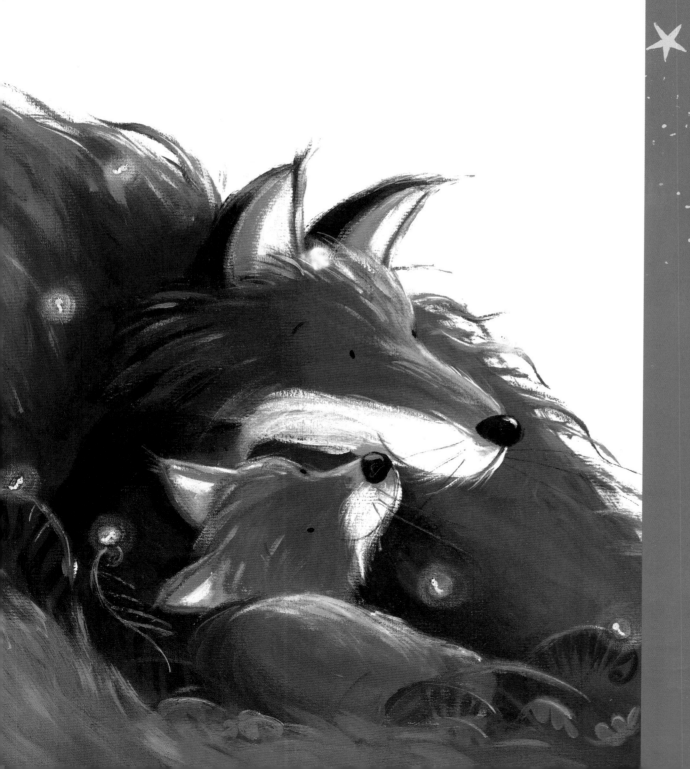

"And it starts right here . . .

". . . with my own little star."